HAPPY

READING !

FRANCES

About the Author

Phil Barnes is a new author, *My Teacher's a Spy!* is his second book in the *My Teacher* Series. He is an imaginative dreamer who loves to write and read.

Phil hopes you enjoy his books as much as he enjoys writing them.

Dedication

I would like to dedicate this book to my late brother-in-law, Jeff Hipwood, who would have loved the *My Teacher* Series, been proud and supportive as he loved to read himself.

I would also like to thank my wife, Lindsay, and my sons, Will and Sam. As well as friends and work colleagues for their continued support, you know who you are!

Phil Barnes

My Teacher's A
SPY!

AUSTIN MACAULEY
PUBLISHERS LTD.

A CIP catalogue record for this title is available from the British Library.

ISBN 9781786294975 (Paperback)
ISBN 9781786294982 (Hardback)
ISBN 9781786294999 (E-Book)

www.austinmacauley.com

First Published (2017)
Austin Macauley Publishers Ltd.
25 Canada Square
Canary Wharf
London
E14 5LQ

Chapter 1

Memories of Christmas were fading fast, presents, Christmas dinner and the family together seemed to be becoming a thing of the past already. Though it had not snowed yet and by the look of the early morning sky was threatening to do so at any time, it was still bitterly cold and upon seeing your breath in the air made it feel colder. Chloe walked to school with her mum whilst her younger brother Archie lagged behind praying for snow, Chloe didn't usually walk with her mum and brother to school but today was the start of a new term and her mum liked to take them on day one.

With the holidays over and a new school term about to begin, Chloe was excited to be able to see her friends and exchange gossip whilst comparing Christmas presents. She had spoken to Jessica and Kelly during the holidays but nothing beat getting back together, she had known them since day one of school and now they were in Year 6, 11 years old and would be moving up to Senior School in September.

"Come on Archie," called Mum for about the dozenth time already, "we'll be late at this rate." Chloe shook her head wondering how her and Archie were related, they were nothing alike and never agreed on anything but he did make her laugh, in fact he made everyone laugh, *he was contagious* she thought and smiled whilst he caught up.

"Right, now let's get a move on," said Mum.

"Will it snow today?" asked Archie.

"Looks very likely," Mum replied, the grin on Archie's face spread from ear to ear and he started to list all the things he would do in the snow before the day was out. Chloe was not bothered about the snow, she felt she was too old to be running around in the snow, making snowmen and sledging.

Getting back to normal school life was appealing after the laziness of Christmas, Chloe hated being sat around doing nothing, her brain was always on the go and she had an active imagination. They reached the school gates with a couple of minutes to spare and upon reaching the gate Jessica, Kelly and Andrew were waiting for her, Andrew was the fourth friend in their gang, he wasn't like other boys, he was not bothered about football but instead loved to write and like the three girls had a very vivid imagination.

Archie ran off as soon as they were through the gate before mum had a chance to kiss him goodbye, Chloe said her goodbyes and joined her friends, *let the gossiping commence* she thought as Jessica turned to the group, "I've heard a rumour that we have a new teacher in school," she started.

"Really," said Kelly.

"It's true," Andrew added, "I saw a new car in the teachers' car park this morning, a black golf."

"You and cars," said Chloe, "doesn't mean we have a new teacher, could be an old teacher with a new car." Before anyone could answer the bell sounded to indicate the start of the new day, "We will see," said Andrew, "we will see..."

Chapter 2

As the friends made their way in to class the school was buzzing as children exchanged gossip, compared Christmas presents and laughed with friends they had not seen for a couple of weeks. The register was completed quickly and the class began to settle in for the new school term but before they had got ready for the first lesson of the day Miss Edwards addressed the class.

"Class," she began, "I know we normally have assembly on a Friday but today there are some important announcements, so if you could follow me quietly to the hall for morning assembly." Everyone rose from their seats, Chloe looked at Andrew who wore a smug grin on his face as if to say I told you so, she smiled back thinking *Andrew is nosier and gossips more than anyone I've ever met.*

They made their way to the hall as all the classes in school did and took their seats on the benches at the back, being in Year 6 had this one advantage in assembly but being slightly higher up than the rest of the school meant not only greater comfort but you also got noticed easily, which they had found out a few times and had been told off for talking during assembly. Chloe remembered easier days when they would talk and laugh during assembly whilst enjoying the cover of being hidden amongst Years 3, 4 and 5 sat crossed legged on the floor, she sighed and squidged up closer to Jessica.

Once everyone was seated quietly in the hall the Deputy Head Teacher Mrs Poole came up on to the slightly raised stage area and spoke.

"Good morning everyone."

"Good morning, Mrs Poole," came the reply.

"I hope you all had a wonderful Christmas but I trust you are ready for the new term ahead."

A few mumblings and some nodding of heads broke out amongst the children.

"Get on with it," Andrew whispered trying to look almost ventriloquist like, not moving his lips, a few children suppressed giggles at this and then Mrs Poole continued.

"I have two important announcements to make," at this Chloe and her friends sat forward, interested.

"Firstly, Mr Jones will not be with us for six to eight weeks, he had a small accident over Christmas and will need some rest."

Again, mumblings broke out amongst the children as they tried to guess what had happened or make up their own funny versions to amuse each other.

"When you have quite finished," said Mrs Poole a bit louder, a hush came over the children and Mrs Poole continued, "so I would like to welcome Mr Gunning, who will be taking over whilst Mr Jones is recovering."

At that Mr Gunning walked in to the hall and on to the stage, he was tall, blond and seemed full of confidence, "Please welcome Mr Gunning and give him every courtesy you give all the teachers," Mrs Poole finished as she stepped aside.

"Well, good morning," Mr Gunning said grinning whilst all the while scanning everyone in the hall.

Chapter 3

A deathly silence had filled the hall as all the children stared at Mr Gunning, he was very handsome with deep blue eyes that seemed to penetrate right through you and make you feel vulnerable but at the same time trusting like you could tell him all your secrets without regret.

After a long pause Mr Gunning spoke, "I am looking forward to meeting and working with everyone during my short time here." Again he looked around as if he were scanning the room and taking in every piece of information, a couple of girls from Year 6 blushed when his eyes fell on them, even a teacher from Year 3, Miss Mills, went red and looked embarrassed when he finished scanning and stopped at her.

The short assembly finished with Mrs Poole again welcoming Mr Gunning and dismissing the children from the hall, upon leaving the hall the noise level began to rise as the children started to talk about Mr Gunning and began to form their opinions of him.

Girls from Year 6 giggled and talked about how fit Mr Gunning was, other children talked about what he meant with meeting everyone, does that mean he will take lessons or join in was a regular question asked.

Teachers hushed their pupils and led them back to class, Chloe nudged Kelly, "What do you think?" she whispered.

"Oh, he's very good looking," Kelly replied.

"Not that," Chloe hissed.

"Oh," Kelly responded going slightly red.

"I mean, do you think something funny is going on?" Chloe whispered.

"I do," Andrew interrupted, "he looks like an actor to me," he finished not bothering to lower his voice, "Andrew," Miss Edwards called, "hush now." Andrew nodded in obedience and turned to the girls with a sheepish grin on his face.

"Well, whatever he's here for let's make a point of finding out," Chloe said quietly not daring to anger Miss Edwards, Jessica nodded and added, "I agree, he does remind me of an actor."

"We'll keep an eye on him," Andrew added and they entered their classroom, found their seats and agreed to talk again later.

First lesson was shorter than normal due to the hastily called assembly and before they knew it they were going out for break, the gang got together on the playground and began to discuss the morning's events.

"I think an actor is right," Andrew started. "Perhaps he is here for some research."

"But why not tell us?" Kelly asked.

"Good point," Jessica added.

"To stay undercover and get the best results," Andrew uttered quickly.

"Makes sense," Chloe said absently whilst thinking.

"You have an answer for everything," Kelly said to Andrew who stood looking pleased with himself, *not for the first time today* Chloe thought. "You know …" Chloe started, "smugness is quite an ugly trait." at this Andrew sagged, the girls laughed, Andrew puffed out his cheeks "whatever," he said and they all laughed again ...

Chapter 4

The rest of the day passed without incident but the talk of the school was still Mr Gunning and stories of how Mr Jones had been in an accident, as with all gossip Mr Jones had done everything from falling off Mount Everest to being attacked by a shark whilst scuba diving. Chloe had heard enough stories for a lifetime but had to laugh at some and considering how simple the explanation probably was made them all the more entertaining.

Andrew was absolutely sure he was right as usual and that Mr Gunning was an actor researching a role with the school agreeing to help, he told the girls he intended to get some answers and would begin poking around after school.

"What are you going to do?" asked Jessica as they left the classroom.

"I think I will start with his car," Andrew said.

"Why?" asked Kelly.

"A car can tell you a lot about a person," Andrew began, "and as I only got a glimpse this morning I will need to get a better look."

"Well, don't be too obvious," said Chloe, and then she quickly added, "do you need some look outs?"

"That would be wise," Andrew replied and they made their way to the teachers' car park. They found the car and waited, Andrew carefully approached and gave it a once over, he peered in the window, the car was neat and tidy, perfectly maintained and spotless inside and out.

Very nice Andrew thought as he went towards the driver's window to investigate further, with his face almost pressed against the glass he peered in, after what seemed an age he stood up with a confused look and turned to the girls.

"What is it?" Chloe whispered loudly but before she got an answer Kelly started to whistle, this was the signal and Andrew darted over to them.

They stood quietly on the field next to the car park and Kelly joined them trying to remain inconspicuous and not look at the car or Mr Gunning who was approaching it rapidly. They watched him click the fob and the car sprang to life, he opened the door, jumped in, adjusted the mirrors and started the engine, they watched carefully trying not to get noticed and then off he went quickly and smoothly out of the school gate.

"That's some car," Andrew said rapidly as if he had been holding his breath the whole time.

"What do you mean?" Jessica asked.

"I have never seen so many dials on the dashboard before, must be really new, I think I will search the internet later but it's way more advanced than I have ever seen."

"Well, you're the expert," Chloe said, "text me later if you find out anything interesting," she added as they started to leave school.

"I'm not sure if he is an actor now," Andrew said as he trotted behind the three girls.

"I think you're right," replied Chloe, "so who is he then and what is he doing here …?" she added looking round at her friends, they all shrugged but each was determined to find out.

Chapter 5

The following morning at school Chloe found her friends waiting at the school gate whispering, "What is it?" Chloe asked as she joined them.

"I was just saying, I've never seen anything like that car before, I looked over countless pages on the internet last night, this car is so new, like yesterday new," Andrew said quietly.

"I was wondering why you didn't text me," Chloe said in return

"Sorry, not a lot to say really," Andrew replied whilst shrugging.

"So what now?" Jessica asked looking at her friends in turn.

"I want another look at that car," Andrew said and he started to walk towards the teachers' car park.

"Hold on," Kelly called behind him, "you'll need back up," she added.

They quickly made their way round to the car park, as expected Mr Gunning's car was parked up neatly, Andrew approached but then stopped dead in his tracks, the three girls had not expected this and walked straight into the back of Andrew and they all stumbled forward. "What the…" Chloe began but she noticed Andrew's confused face, he looked like he was multiplying the largest sum ever invented and was struggling to come up with an answer.

"What's wrong?" Jessica asked.

"But ..." was all Andrew uttered and an Andrew lost for words was something the girls had never seen before.

"But what?" Chloe asked.

"But how...?" was all he could say in reply.

"I don't get it," Kelly said impatiently. "But what, but how, what is he going on about?" she added, the girls stared at the car and then back at Andrew but could not understand his confusion.

Suddenly Andrew came back to life, "That's not possible," he said.

"What?" all three girls said together in equal frustration.

"Look at the number plate," he urged and pointed at the car's yellow number plate but to the girls there was nothing wrong and they turned to Andrew with puzzled looks.

"Yesterday the number plate was BG12 THE and now its GB21 HET, number plates don't change, that's against the law," Andrew said hurriedly as he shook his head,

"Oh," said Chloe, "I never noticed that."

"No one looks at the number plate," Andrew said "but it's the most important part, it tells you important information."

"This is getting weird ..." Jessica said.

"Let's get going before we are noticed," added Kelly as she looked around.

They made their way round to class, the bell sounded and children began to filter in to school, "This is strange," whispered Chloe "a car with changing number plates, Mr Jones suddenly off sick, Mr Gunning taking over out of the blue ..." she continued, the others nodded in agreement.

"He is definitely up to something and we need to know what," Jessica whispered back. They got to class and found their seats ready for the day ahead but determined to uncover the truth about Mr Gunning...

Chapter 6

"Chloe, Chloe, Chloe," Miss Edwards repeated getting louder each time, Jessica nudged Chloe for a second time but harder than before.

"Ow, what did you ..." Chloe began before trailing off as she realised that Miss Edwards was staring at her, then she noticed the whole class staring and she went bright red with embarrassment before uttering, "Yes Miss Edwards ..."

"I was asking you a question," Miss Edwards said.

"Sorry," replied Chloe, she had been a million miles away, totally pre-occupied with why Mr Gunning was at their school and trying to work out a way of finding out.

Chloe was relieved when break came, she darted out of the classroom and in to the playground, Jessica and Kelly joined her still giggling.

"It's not funny," said Chloe.

"Sorry," replied the girls as Andrew joined them.

"What's up with you?" he asked Chloe with a grin on his face.

"I was thinking about Mr Gunning and his car with the changing plate," said Chloe defensively.

"Oh," Jessica and Kelly said together.

"Thought so," added Andrew nodding as if in agreement.

"Whilst I was leaving class I heard Miss Edwards tell Maria that Mr Gunning would be involved in our lesson before lunch," he said proudly as if delivering an acceptance speech,

"Really ..." said Chloe, "now that's great news."

"Why?" asked Kelly.

"So we can watch and question him," said Jessica interrupting whilst looking at Chloe for agreement, Chloe nodded and they began whispering all at once with ideas and questions they would put to Mr Gunning.

The lesson before lunch was Design Technology and they would be starting new projects, the children got together in groups of four to discuss ideas on a project, Miss Edwards let them decide their own projects whilst Mr Gunning quietly walked around the room listening and joining in with different group discussions.

"That's a great idea," Chloe blurted out loudly, "a listening device or eaves dropper is brilliant," she added.

"How do we make that?" asked Jessica but before anyone could say a word Mr Gunning jumped in.

"Well, it's quite simple really," he began, "a small amplifier, head phones, battery, a few wires and hey presto ... an eaves dropper," he finished.

The girls all grinned whilst Andrew thought about it and then added, "You seem to know a lot about it," at that Mr Gunning stuttered slightly.

"Well, yes, not really. Saw a program on TV about it ..." he said quickly and moved to the next table rapidly before looking back at the gang and eyeing them suspiciously.

Andrew stood triumphantly, smiling at the girls, "What?" hissed Kelly.

"I know what he is," said Andrew confidently.

But before he could utter another word Chloe whispered to the group, "A Spy…"

Chapter 7

"A …" started Kelly.

"Shush," Chloe said and she put her hand over Kelly's mouth to stop her from finishing, "yes, a Spy," she whispered.

"The evidence is there, with what just happened and the advanced car with the changing number plate," Andrew added, his triumphant demeanour lost after Chloe had stolen his thunder.

Kelly exchanged looks with Jessica who started to nod, "it all makes sense," she said quietly and Kelly looked around at her three friends and mouthed "Wow."

As the lesson came to an end Mr Gunning thanked Miss Edwards and began to leave, as he passed the desk where Chloe and the gang were packing up Andrew said, "Nice car, Sir."

Mr Gunning stopped and turned to Andrew.

"Thank you," he said slowly and Andrew gave him the most obvious wink, Mr Gunning looked at him a bit perplexed, then he left in a hurry, Chloe nudged Andrew.

"What was that?"

"What?" Andrew replied and the girls just shook their heads.

"What do we do now then?" asked Jessica as they sat in the playground after scoffing lunch, "I don't know yet," said Chloe pensively.

"We need to watch his movements," said Andrew, "see what he does, where he goes and who he talks to," he added, the girls nodded in agreement but how they would do this this none of them knew.

"From what I've heard from other classes, Mr Gunning likes to take part in lessons and has sat in some today and yesterday," Jessica said.

"He doesn't hang around," said Andrew.

"For now let's just see how many classes he takes part in and then ask some discreet questions," Chloe added looking straight at Andrew.

"What?" said Andrew defensively, "I can be discreet."

"Prove it," replied Chloe.

"You've got the biggest mouth in school," Kelly added, Jessica nodded in agreement whilst Andrew looked at the floor feeling a little uncomfortable.

Afternoon lessons were passing as normal in 6E, Miss Edwards was explaining a maths problem to the class when there was a knock at the door and Mr Gunning entered, "Sorry to disturb you in full flow, Miss Edwards, but may I borrow Chloe White?" Miss Edwards blushed slightly.

"Of course, anything we can do to help," she said and then realised the class were staring at her and she quickly turned away embarrassed.

"Chloe ..." Mr Gunning said as he smiled and motioned for her to follow him out, Chloe slowly rose to her feet and glanced round the table at her friends who all exchanged puzzled looks and shrugged. She made her way out of the classroom and followed Mr Gunning but to her surprise it was not towards the Head Teacher's Office but outside and on to the playing field, "Put this on," he said and handed her a very bright yellow high visibility jacket.

Chloe looked at him very puzzled and said, "Have I done something wrong, Sir?"

Mr Gunning passed her a litter grabber; he held a rubbish bag and started walking, "Sir ..." Chloe said quietly, Mr Gunning looked round.

"This is cover, Chloe so no one can hear or suspect anything, you seem to be the leader of your clever gang."

Chloe nodded nervously, "Don't panic, Chloe," began Mr Gunning, "now, why do you think I'm here?"

"We think ..." she began but stopped herself; "we think you ..." she tried again.

"Go on," said Mr Gunning enthusiastically.

"We think you're a Spy," she spat out quicker than she had meant to.

Mr Gunning grinned, "Chloe White, sister of Archie, daughter of Mike and Ellen, lives in Hopewell Street, family car is green, your last holiday was to Mallorca, you have grandparents who live in Cork and your pet, well Archie's pet rat is called Oscar." Chloe stopped and stared open mouthed, "Yes, Chloe, I am a Spy and I would like your help ..."

Chapter 8

Chloe stood staring at Mr Gunning still open mouthed, though her and her friends had considered Mr Gunning was a Spy to be told it by Mr Gunning himself was still a revelation. "Stop gaping and carry on as normal," Mr Gunning said softly.

"Sorry," muttered Chloe, "but though we suspected something was strange, I am still stunned," she added.

"I would like you and your friends to help me," he said and then became serious before continuing, "Only you, Jessica, Kelly and Andrew will have this information, so please keep it to yourselves."

Chloe nodded still in disbelief at what she was hearing, "there is a teacher here that is the head of a criminal gang, they have concealed themselves very well so it could be any teacher who has worked here for two years or less, which discounts a lot but also leaves quite a few—"

"Yes," Chloe interrupted "Mrs Poole, the Secretary Mrs Jones and all the lunch time staff have all been here for years."

"Very good Chloe," Mr Gunning replied, Chloe smiled back, "I have a list of possibles but need more information," he added.

"What can we do?" asked Chloe trying to remain steady and not get too excited.

"As you may have heard there have been a lot of car thefts and home burglaries in the last two years."

"That's right," Chloe added, "Stephen's parents had their brand new car stolen just before Christmas."

Mr Gunning smiled at Chloe but carried on walking as Chloe picked up rubbish to make the ruse look like an ordinary punishment, "It would seem this teacher plans cleverly, new cars go missing quick and houses are robbed when the family is on holiday, being a teacher gives them access to this information very easily and we need to figure out who this is, then put a stop to it," Mr Gunning said.

Chloe was almost bursting with excitement, she could not wait to tell the gang but her head was also filled with possible suspects, "Mr Gunning, would you like us to start poking around and asking questions, no one would suspect a child to be on to them."

"Good idea, Chloe, but please be careful this criminal is very cunning which is why I have been brought in, the police have tried and failed, so it's up to us now," he said quietly and calmly.

"I won't let you down," she answered proudly, "I will speak with the gang and we will tread carefully and report anything we find out."

"Thank you, Chloe, I also need you to carefully spread around to as many children as possible that they should not tell anyone about holidays booked or new cars bought, I am starting to approve holiday's myself so Mrs Jones will collect this information then hopefully this will pull the criminal out of their comfort zone, but please be discreet."

"Don't worry, we are very clever, Mr Gunning," she replied smiling.

"I know," he said in return, "that I figured out very quickly," and he winked at her, gave her a big smile and said, "that's enough litter picking for today, let's get back in now."

Chapter 9

Chloe raced back to class after walking in to school with Mr Gunning, her heart was pounding and she couldn't wait to tell the others what had just happened. As she entered the classroom everyone turned to see who came in, most went back to their work but Jessica, Kelly and Andrew stared at Chloe, "Well, don't just stand there," Miss Edwards began, "go back to your desk and continue where you left off," she finished.

Chloe grinned sheepishly and did as she was told, as she sat down the others looked at her expectantly, "After school," she hissed quietly, Jessica and Kelly nodded but Andrew still looked at Chloe, she nodded at his work and shook her head slightly, "not now," she mouthed to him, Andrew looked on dejected but did as she said.

As they were leaving school Andrew was getting impatient, "Come on, Chloe, this is killing me ... please," he begged.

"In a minute," she replied almost enjoying the suspense too much, as they started to leave the school gates behind Chloe began.

"Mr Gunning is most definitely a Spy," she started.

"I knew it," shouted Andrew whilst the others looked at him shaking their heads, "sorry, but I did," he answered softly.

"Zip it Andrew and let Chloe speak," Jessica said getting a bit annoyed with him. Andrew shrugged apologetically and then Chloe told them all that had happened, what Mr Gunning had said and to make sure that his cover was kept secret.

"That's unbelievable," said Kelly.

"A real life Spy in our school," Jessica added.

"More importantly a real life Criminal Mastermind," Andrew said interrupting.

"What next then?" Kelly asked. Chloe thought for a moment then started.

"We must tread carefully," the others nodded then she added, "First I think we start spreading the word about holidays and cars ... discreetly, Andrew." He looked on a bit embarrassed but nodded in agreement.

"Come round to mine tonight and we will draw up a list of possibilities and a list of definite no's," said Chloe, they all agreed this was a good place to start and off they trotted home full of excitement.

That evening at Chloe's they secretly and quietly started to make lists, "We can rule out the following ..." Chloe began, "Mrs Poole, the Secretary Mrs Jones, all the catering staff, Mr Gough and Mrs Locke."

"Why all the catering staff?" asked Kelly.

"Mr Gunning is positive it's a teacher as they have access to the information needed and they have been here for years," Chloe replied.

"I see," Kelly said then added, "also you can add Mrs Parker, Mrs Collins and Mr Bishop, they have been here years as well."

Silently they thought on, "Ah, Miss Presley is another," Andrew blurted out.

"Any more?" Chloe asked looking at her friends.

"Miss Bennett," said Jessica, "I remember her teaching my older brother John."

"Good," said Chloe, "so, that leaves these as our suspects," she added after a long pause.

"Miss Edwards, Miss Phelps, Miss Oliver, Mr Baxter, Miss Barker, Mr Young, Mrs Long, Miss Wilson and Miss Dobbs ..." she said slowly as she wrote each one down then looked up at her friends who were all grinning with excitement.

"Let's get spying ..." whispered Andrew and they all giggled nervously.

Chapter 10

For the next two days the gang worked carefully and quietly as they continued to poke around, watching the teachers on their list and casually spreading the word around school about keeping quiet about new cars and holidays.

Andrew was already convinced that the criminal was Mr Baxter, "What makes you think it's him?" asked Kelly on Friday afternoon.

"He looks suspicious and has a very expensive car," said Andrew in defence.

"So?" replied Kelly.

"So ..." began Andrew, "that means he has money, cars don't grow on trees."

"Well, I think Mr Young could be the one, he is quite strange and always seems to be everywhere," said Jessica quietly as she chewed the top of her pencil.

"I'm not sure yet," chipped in Chloe, "but I'm positive it's not Miss Edwards, Miss Barker or Miss Dobbs, they are all too nice," she finished.

The others nodded in agreement with Kelly adding, "And Miss Oliver, she can't control her class let alone a criminal gang," and they all laughed.

The weekend was slow and dragged, Chloe was desperate to get back to school, the snow Archie had yearned for never turned up and he was moaning at being bored whilst annoying everyone else.

Chloe sat in her room looking at the list of suspects slowly drumming her fingers on the desk, Mr Baxter or Mrs Long she said softly to herself, they seem to be the prime suspects, clever, organised and respected she continued lost in a world of her own, *but which one* she thought.

Monday morning had not come quick enough, Chloe rushed to school early to see her friends, she wasn't disappointed as Jessica and Kelly were already waiting for her, "Andrew?" she asked.

"Not seen him yet," answered Jessica.

"I think I have got it down to two," said Chloe, "Mr Baxter and Mrs Long." Kelly and Jessica exchanged looks and both said, "Me too," before looking at each other again and laughing.

"Me three," said a voice behind them, Andrew had just turned up and heard what was going on.

"They seem the two most likely don't they?" Chloe said whilst her friends nodded, "I will go to Mr Gunning," she added, "and report what we think."

During first break Chloe found Mr Gunning and told him what the gang had come up whilst explaining why they thought these two were good suspects, "So you see," Chloe stated, "both are clever, well organised and respected around school."

"Very good," Mr Gunning replied. "I will check these two out then," and he strolled off before she could say another word. Chloe found the gang; she had a proud smile on her face which told them all they needed to know.

"Mr Gunning was pleased," Chloe started, "but I think we need more."

"Another car theft happened over the weekend," Andrew said, "Daniel Doyle from Year 5. His parents had their brand new Range Rover stolen on Sunday."

"Good," Kelly said, "well not good for Daniel, but for our interests any way," she added.

"Okay," said Chloe, "but we need to find out more," she added before they were interrupted by the bell to end break.

Chapter 11

"No ..." Chloe hissed at Andrew during afternoon lesson, "Mr Gunning will check them out and get back to us," she continued.

"Besides, you don't want to be caught following a suspect do you?" added Jessica, Andrew thought for a minute but before he could answer there was a tap on his shoulder.

He turned to see Miss Edwards standing beside their desk, she looked cross and the gang shrank back in to their chairs, "Whispering ... constant whispering," said Miss Edwards, "something you would like to share?" and looked round at the four red faces who all just shook their heads. "Any more of this nonsense and there will be dinner time detention, is that clear?" said Miss Edwards.

All four nodded and Chloe replied with a weak, "Yes, sorry Miss."

Miss Edwards walked back to her desk eyeing the gang one last time before sitting down; they all looked at each other and then got on with their work without another word being uttered for the remainder of the day.

Leaving the school gates behind Chloe opened her mouth to talk but was beaten by Kelly, "You're going to get us all in trouble," she said looking straight at Andrew, he looked down at his feet and kicked at the floor nervously.

"We have to stop talking about this in class," said Chloe after an awkward silence. "We can't be overheard or else it could ruin everything," she finished, her friends nodded in agreement. "Right, my house at 6 p.m. tonight then," she said and they split up to make their way home.

It was 6.20 p.m. and for the dozenth time Jessica rang Kelly's phone but only got the answering machine again, she looked at Chloe and Andrew with concern, "She's never late," said Jessica softly.

"It's alright," replied Chloe, "I'm sure she's fine," but she too was concerned as Kelly was never late and always had her phone on her, she was practically glued to the phone every chance she got.

"What now?" said Andrew, breaking the silence. Chloe and Jessica shrugged.

"Try her home number," said Chloe, Jessica rang but was greeted with the answer machine.

"Shall we go round?" asked Andrew nervously, he was feeling a little guilty after what Kelly had said after school.

What if we have been overheard by someone, but they wouldn't harm any of us would they? thought Chloe.

"Let's forget about it for tonight, I can't think straight now," said Chloe, her two friends nodded, Jessica looked close to tears but got up with Andrew to leave. As they left Chloe's room the home phone rang and Chloe's mum answered but they thought nothing of it as their concern for Kelly was starting to overwhelm them, Chloe was saying goodbye at the back door when her mum called her, "Hang on a minute, I'm just seeing Jessica and Andrew out," she called back

"Bring them too," replied her mum.

Confused, the three found Chloe's mum, "That was Kelly's mum on the phone, Kelly has been in an accident and is in hospital," she said, Chloe, Jessica and Andrew looked horrified. "Don't panic," she continued, "it's a broken leg, broken arm and some scratches, she will be fine," she finished but she got no response just the same horrified look and then Jessica started to cry ....

Chapter 12

News of Kelly's accident was all the school was talking about the next day, how these things spread so fast Chloe knew not as she sat in class during first lesson. She looked at the empty seat where Kelly usually sat with sadness and then she caught Jessica's eye, but looked away just as quick as she was sure Jessica would start to cry again given the encouragement.

Chloe's mum explained that Kelly had been hit by a car in what was called 'a hit and run', where the car never stopped, she had been on her way home from school and had not long left her friends. Chloe felt angry at this and was beginning to suspect foul play. Morning break arrived swiftly, the gang met in the playground to talk, "I'm worried," began Chloe.

"What do you mean?" asked Jessica.

"I do not think this was an accident," she replied.

"You think this was intentional?" Andrew blurted out.

"I do, and I will ask Mr Gunning for his thoughts," she finished and strolled off before another word could be uttered.

"I don't know about that," Mr Gunning said to Chloe, "accidents like this do happen, I think she was unfortunate and luckily was only just caught at a slow speed but I will investigate to put your mind at rest," he finished. Chloe smiled and started to leave, but Mr Gunning whispered loudly, "Please be careful." She nodded and walked away.

That evening they visited Kelly in Hospital, all three relieved to see her sat up talking as normal but with leg and arm plastered, cuts and bruises over her face and her other arm bandaged around the wrist. "I didn't see them coming," Kelly said as she described what she could remember, "it happened so quick, I was just crossing the road round the corner from where I left you guys but I remember seeing a black Jeep type thing driving away, I got a blurry photo on my phone but not enough for the Police to go on," she finished.

"We're just glad you're okay," said Chloe.

"I was worried sick," added Jessica with a lump in her throat and she swallowed back the tears before they had a chance to flow again.

"Must have been terrifying," added Chloe trying to move the conversation on.

"I've never broken a bone before this and now two, along with a sprained wrist," Kelly said nodding at her injuries, "be the first to sign my cast," she added looking round at her friends.

Jessica brightened as they began to decorate Kelly's casts with silly things, then Andrew said, "Where's that photo then?"

"Oh yeah, on my phone, just there," and she nodded at the table.

Andrew picked it up and before he unlocked it Kelly said, "Photo only, I know how nosey you are." Chloe and Jessica laughed while a sheepish Andrew looked at the picture.

"That's the Range Rover," Andrew shouted out.

"Ssshhhh," said Chloe then added, "what Range Rover?"

"This is the Range Rover stolen from Daniel Doyle's parents at the weekend," he said quietly and the girls stared at him whilst turning white as a sheet ...

Chapter 13

After what seemed an eternity Chloe whispered slowly, "Are you sure, Andrew?" Andrew nodded as if in slow motion, Jessica and Kelly exchanged nervous glances, with Jessica close to tears again. Chloe spoke, "It could be a coincidence, it doesn't mean Kelly was targeted," she said trying to convince herself as much as the others.

No one spoke for a while, Andrew studied the photo over and over, Jessica looked at Kelly trying to smile reassuringly whilst Chloe paced around the small Hospital room. The silence was broken suddenly by Kelly's mum entering the room abruptly, the door opened loudly making the four of them jump, "Right, visiting time is over I'm afraid," said Kelly's mum as she began to usher them out. Chloe looked back at Kelly who was still looking deathly white and smiled nervously before mouthing, "It's okay, don't panic," which was easier to say than do, they all felt sick and though no one would admit it, they had been found out.

The following day Chloe met Jessica and Andrew at the school gate, she had hardly slept that night and she was trying her best to keep herself together, "What are we going to do?" asked Jessica looking to Chloe for answers. Andrew, too, stared at her anxiously awaiting her response.

"I will go and speak to Mr Gunning, he'll know what to do," Chloe said smiling weakly and she turned away towards school hoping her friends had not seen how she really felt.

At break time Chloe searched the playground for Mr Gunning but she was left wanting as he was nowhere to be seen, she checked the car park and had that horrible sinking feeling when she realised his car wasn't there, *oh no* she thought *what now* ...

On her way back in to class she found Jessica and Andrew, "We are on our own," she said quietly.

"What!" both Jessica and Andrew said together.

"Mr Gunning is not here today," Chloe said in reply.

"Okay, okay," started Andrew "we just stay together and act normal."

"We'll be fine," added Chloe as they sat at their desk, "no one is going to harm us, I'm sure," she finished, though she didn't know that for sure and that worried her; she glanced around class looking for something out of place or something unusual but all seemed normal.

The rest of the school day was torment for the three friends, constant nervousness, looking over their shoulders and paranoia was all they had, things had taken a wrong turn, Kelly had been targeted because of their poking around and was in Hospital, Mr Gunning was nowhere to be found and they were losing their minds...

Chapter 14

The following day at school and Mr Gunning was still nowhere to be seen; the friends had wanted to visit Kelly in Hospital again but were told she needed her rest much to their frustration.

"We have to do something," whispered Andrew as they made their way to the hall for morning assembly.

"What can we do?" Jessica whispered back.

"I don't know, anything to try and catch the criminal out," replied Andrew exasperated and nearly losing control of his hushed tone.

Jessica was silent for a moment then she looked at Andrew with pity and said, "We are only children, Andrew, Kelly has ended up in Hospital and Mr Gunning has vanished, give it up …"

Andrew looked mortified and was about to respond but was interrupted by Chloe who had been quietly listening to their conversation, "I think I may have a plan," she uttered slowly and almost silently enough that Andrew and Jessica had to lean in closer. "I will tell you at break," she added and carefully looked around to spot any eavesdroppers, Andrew looked at her imploringly but she remained stout and took her seat in the hall.

"Good morning, everyone," said Mrs Poole loudly, after getting a response she liked she carried on, "some of you may have noticed that Mr Gunning was not here yesterday, unfortunately he has had a family emergency to tend with and we hope to see him soon." Jessica and Chloe looked up, suspicion tingling through their bodies whilst Andrew casually scanned the teachers for anything odd but was left disappointed.

The assembly continued but all Chloe could think of was Mr Gunning, *where are you* she thought *we need you* and before she knew it everyone was starting to leave the hall and go back to class, things were getting desperate, Chloe had the makings of a plan but this could be dangerous now, especially after what had happened to Kelly and she did not want to put Jessica or Andrew in jeopardy.

Morning break arrived swiftly and the three friends found a quiet spot on the playground, "Come on then," said Andrew eagerly.

"Yes," started Jessica, "what is this plan you have?" Chloe sat down, looked at her friends and began.

"The way I see it we only have one choice and that is to see this through to the end." Andrew and Jessica looked at Chloe, neither spoke but both nodded gravely, "we need to set a trap, we must see who turns up and try to gather information, like who it is, where they go ..." Chloe looked at Andrew who was waiting to interrupt.

"Yes," he began, "we can take some pictures and I can follow whoever shows up."

"That might be dangerous," Jessica chipped in looking worried

"I'll be careful," added Andrew looking at Jessica.

"Firstly," started Chloe, "we need to find somewhere to set the trap and then start the game of whispers, nothing stays quiet or secret in this school."

"Your house tonight?" asked Andrew, Chloe nodded.

Chapter 15

That evening Chloe was sitting in her room waiting for Andrew and Jessica, absently she was tapping a pen against her head hoping she was doing the right thing, hoping no harm would come to her friends.

Andrew arrived dead on 6 p.m. with Jessica a couple of minutes later, once all together they closed the bedroom door and began to discuss what they would do.

"The car part is easy," began Chloe, "you know Robbie who lives just down from you, Jess." Jessica nodded, "well," Chloe continued, "he has never been able to keep quiet and I heard him telling Simon that his neighbour has just bought a brand new Jaguar, now Simon doesn't say much but we could spread that news a bit faster." Andrew smiled.

"Then we could watch from your house," he said looking at Jessica who looked a bit uncomfortable. "I have some walkie-talkies as well," Andrew added excitedly.

"That's it then, we spread the Jaguar news fast and then straight from school to Jess's house and watch," Chloe said, Andrew nodded in agreement and Jessica said:

"Yes," quietly before adding, "we're not going to do anything stupid, are we?"

Next day at school the three of them spread the Jaguar news like their lives depended on it, there was still no sign of Mr Gunning but with their plan in motion their thoughts were preoccupied and they did not have time to worry where he had got to.

No sooner had the bell for the end of school rung than Chloe had practically leapt from her seat and was out of the door with Andrew and Jessica running behind, "Come on!" she yelled as they left the playground behind, within 10 minutes they were at Jessica's house and ready for the stakeout.

An hour dragged by in the slowest manor possible, Jessica yawned whilst Chloe tapped her feet against the wall under the window, the walkie-talkie crackled in to life and Andrew spoke, "Anything from up there?" he asked.

"For the hundredth time, no …" Chloe replied trying to remain calm. Frustration was nagging away at all three of them, Jessica looked down again, the night was drawing in early as it always did this time of year and soon everything would be under the cover of darkness.

"Stupid," Chloe yelled making Jessica jump, "we are stupid, who would steal a car in daylight?" she added, Jessica nodded.

"Never thought of that," she said and relayed this to Andrew and awaited what was sure to be a smart answer as usual. A minute passed, then two, no response from Andrew, "Funny …" said Jessica.

"What is?" asked Chloe.

"I was sure Andrew would come back after that last message I sent," Jessica added.

Chloe frowned and picked up the walkie-talkie, "Andrew, anything from down there?" she said, no reply, a minute passed but still nothing, "Andrew, you okay?"

said Chloe trying to remain calm and not make eye contact with Jessica.

"Andrew, stop messing around," said Chloe laughing softly to mask her fear, "Andrew, come on, very funny," she added, but still no response came, "wait here Jess," Chloe said as she got up.

"Where are you going?" asked Jessica nervously.

Chloe kept walking not daring to face her friend, "To check on Andrew," she replied and she hurried out of the room and down the stairs.

Chloe got to the back door just as Jessica's older brother John came in, "Where you going in such a hurry?" he said as she flew out the door.

"Um, nowhere, back in a minute," she lied and carried on.

"Hold up …" shouted John and he began to follow, Chloe quickly rounded the corner expecting to find Andrew in his hiding spot where she would tell him off for scaring them.

"Oh no …" Chloe exclaimed as she looked down to the floor and saw Andrew's walkie-talkie in bits, tears welled and Chloe was scared, seconds later John came up behind her.

"What's going on?" he said startling Chloe.

She took a breath trying to regain her composure, "Nothing, just a game, Andrew must of dropped this," she said picking up the broken walkie-talkie, John eyed her suspiciously but did not push her any further, Chloe did not dare look at him properly, her insides twisted but she made herself walk back to Jessica's house, *what have I done* she thought, *what have I done, first Kelly and now Andrew, what a mess, what am I going to do now …?*

Chapter 16

Chloe and Jessica sobbed quietly whilst looking at the broken walkie-talkie, another friend was in danger and they had no idea what to do next, Mr Gunning had not been seen in days, they were no closer to finding out who the Criminal Mastermind was and all seemed lost.

"What do we do now?" asked Jessica weakly, her voice crackled as if she were about to cry again, "should we report this to the police?" she continued.

Chloe thought for a moment, dried her eyes and stood up, "NO," she said defiantly, "this will not go on, we carry on just as Andrew would have wanted, he wouldn't give up on us," she said confidently and took Jessica by the hands bringing her to a standing position opposite.

"We fight, Jess, we must," Chloe said looking into Jessica's eyes, Jessica nodded, "Andrew will turn up, they won't harm him, they can't afford to bring attention to themselves or they risk it all going wrong," Chloe said.

"What about Andrew's parents?" Jessica asked.

"We tell them he is staying here tonight, I will stay as well, your parents go to work early, we can cover and your brother John notices nothing, we will fool them for now."

Again Jessica nodded, what else could they do, suddenly the silence was broken by screeching tyres outside, they jumped to the window just in time to see the car they had been watching speed away, Chloe cursed their misfortune but took photo's anyway hoping something might come of them.

Covering for Andrew was easier than they thought, taking three drinks and snacks upstairs and making plenty of noise fooled Jessica's family, *maybe too easy* Jessica thought but the missing of him was very difficult for the girls.

Next morning they dressed for school and waited whilst Jessica's parents left for work; ten minutes later they left shouting good bye to John, Chloe added, "Come on, Andrew, hurry up," for good measure, they had fooled Jessica's family, now on to school, they needed to get something, find a clue or hope Mr Gunning was back as things were getting desperate now.

Morning started as normal with the register and Miss Edwards began calling the names out awaiting a "Yes Miss," reply for every name called, Chloe called out her reply, Jessica followed a few names later, Kelly's was not read out at all which made sense as everyone knew she was in hospital, they waited for the register to end, Andrew was always third from last but his name never came and Miss Edwards closed the red folder on her desk after calling the last name and moved towards the white board to start the days first lesson. Chloe and Jessica exchanged puzzled glances, Jessica was about to say "you missed Andrew," but Chloe stopped her, Jessica looked at her even more puzzled, then it clicked … Jessica gasped and Chloe quickly coughed so no one would hear her.

First lesson dragged by so slowly, but once break arrived Chloe and Jessica found a quiet spot on the playground, "It's Miss Edwards isn't it?" said Jessica stunned by what she had just said.

"It must be …" replied Chloe equally shocked, "no one knew what happened to Andrew apart from us and the criminals," continued Chloe.

"I just can't believe it …" Jessica added, clearly struggling to believe that Miss Edwards was a Criminal Mastermind.

"It has to be, right? Why would she miss his name otherwise, she always reads out every name, never checks who's here before reading it, I'm sure …" Chloe said.

"We need Mr Gunning," replied Jessica.

"I know," said Chloe, but then she had an idea, "Miss Edwards walks to school as she lives so close, I say we hang around and follow her tonight," Chloe said. Jessica looked nervous but nodded, they had nothing to lose now and needed to solve this fast, as terrified as they were they knew what they had to do, *time to stand up and be counted* Chloe thought as they returned to class ….

Chapter 17

For the rest of the day Chloe and Jessica kept very quiet, got on with their lessons and from a distance they watched Miss Edwards still stunned by their discovery, they had been 100% sure it could never be Miss Edwards, they thought she was too nice but the harder Chloe thought about it the more it made sense, she was well liked, organised and respected but most of all very clever.

The school day ended as it began with the school bell ringing three times, Chloe and Jessica slowly rose from their desk at the back of the class, chosen because they were such chatter boxes it hid them well behind their other classmates most of the time. They carefully made their way out of the classroom, slowly but casually making their way to the playground, "Right," Chloe began, "quickly text your mum saying you are coming to mine to do homework and have tea and I will do the same saying I am going to yours." Jessica nodded and they slowly made their way to the school gate.

There they waited, carefully keeping watch, luckily they could still see their classroom window and they watched as Miss Edwards tidied and packed away her belongings, a couple of minutes passed when Jessica suddenly blurted out, "Oh no."

"What?" said Chloe startled.

"What if she uses the other gate, we don't know where she lives only that she walks." Chloe realised their error

"Wait here, I will run round, first to see her follow and text the other," and she was off quick as a flash, leaving Jessica looking worried.

Chloe got to the other gate, a few children still milled around, some lads from Year 5 kicked a ball around, Chloe waited near them hoping to use them as cover should Miss Edwards come this way, sure enough within five minutes Miss Edwards came out of the school, scarf wrapped round looking nothing like a Criminal Mastermind, Chloe was having doubts as she watched Miss Edwards approach the gate, she turned and pretended to be involved with the lads playing football whilst watching Miss Edwards closely.

Chloe texted Jessica, **meet me by dead man's alley**, so named as it was rumoured a man died there a few winters before, **be careful**, she added at the end and then off she went in pursuit of Miss Edwards heart thumping so hard she thought it might burst through her chest, a couple of girls from Year 4 walked in the same direction, Chloe shadowed them hoping that if Miss Edwards did turn round she would not see her.

As they approached dead man's alley the girls from Year 4 turned in a different direction, Chloe cursed but carried on, keeping a bit of distance this time, as she came through the alley Miss Edwards was already half way up Castle Street, Chloe noticed a shape behind a bush, a Jessica-shaped shape, she felt a little better knowing her friend would be by her side again, a minute later and Jessica joined her and they followed into Moat Avenue.

With the Winter nights closing in so quickly the late afternoon gloom was a welcome relief to the girls, they got closer to Miss Edwards but kept deadly quiet, they watched as she turned a corner, slowly they crept up and saw Miss Edwards enter a nice house on the end of Turret Road, "Those houses back on to the old industrial estate," said Jessica, "John used to go there and skateboard." Chloe thought this was interesting.

"Okay, let's check it out," said Chloe and off they went, taking a slight detour to make sure they weren't spotted, they climbed through a hole in the fence, Chloe looked round, plenty of good buildings still standing, the place had been due for demolition a while ago but she had heard people were arguing over what should be built on the site so nothing had happened yet. They decided to look at each building in turn, this was a perfect place to hide stolen goods but they wondered if there was any security.

Carefully they searched the first building, both nervous, hearts pounding but still they carried on, as they came through the first warehouse nothing unusual stood out so they made their way towards the exit, without warning a door slammed loudly behind them, both girls jumped, terrified and looked behind slowly …

Chapter 18

"Oh my," Jessica began her heart beating furiously.

"I know," said Chloe, both breathed a huge sigh of relief, it was just the wind that had blown the door shut, their hearts pounded even harder now, but carefully they made their way through the exit and on to the next warehouse.

As they approached the door to the warehouse they could hear voices, "Quick," Chloe whispered and she dragged Jessica behind some rusty bins, they peered round carefully, "I heard a slam," said a man's voice.

"Let's look in here," said a different voice, the girls heard the men go in the warehouse they had just exited, nothing for a minute, then SLAM, the wind blew the same door shut, the men came out of the slammed door, the smaller man laughed.

"Just a door slamming in the wind," he said chuckling, the bigger man cursed and they carried on walking away.

Chloe got up, "Come on, Jess," she whispered and they followed the men as quietly as possible.

The closer they got the more they could see the men, both were dressed in security clothing, they looked very professional but Chloe had a feeling something was not right and they continued at a distance. The men came to a big warehouse near to where the houses backed on to the site, they stopped, looked round very casually then the small man produced some keys from his pocket and opened the door, both went in, the girls scrambled from their hiding spot in the shadows and found the first window on the side of the warehouse and waited underneath it whilst they calmed themselves.

Slowly Chloe got up from under the window as she stood up she quickly realised she would need something to stand on as the window was quite high, higher than a normal house window, she looked for something to stand on prodding Jessica in to action at the same time. They found an old milk crate not far away and carefully carried it back to the window and set it down in the middle, Chloe took a deep breath and then stood on the crate slowly rising until her eyes got to the ledge and then she peered in.

"Wow," she exclaimed.

"What is it?" Jessica said as loudly as she dared.

"Look for yourself," replied Chloe and moved over on the crate.

"Wow," said Jessica wide eyed, "there has to be 20 cars," she added as they both took in the full extent of what was in front of them.

"The security guard uniforms are clever, looks like they are protecting the site when it is just a clever cover," said Chloe. The cars, all new, shined like they had been carefully looked after, behind the cars they noticed even more stolen items, a pile of electrical goods, TVS, radios, DVD Players and computers of all sorts, "They have been busy," said Chloe.

"What now?" whispered Jessica.

"What now indeed?" said a voice behind them, terror gripped the girls and for what seemed an eternity they just froze there not daring to turn round ...

Chapter 19

Out of the corner of her eye Chloe could see Miss Edwards stood behind them, "Run!" she yelled, she split to the right and dashed down the alley between warehouses, she looked over her shoulder but to her horror Miss Edwards had caught Jessica by the hood of her coat. Jessica's feet scrambled as she tried to wriggle free, Chloe rounded the corner and hid between some old bins.

Chloe reached for her phone, *now it's time to call the police* she thought, after checking her pockets she realised she had put her phone in her school bag which she had left on the ground under the window, "What now?" she whispered to herself, back round the corner she heard the sound of voices but did not know what to do so she sat there trying not to panic.

Meanwhile Jessica had stopped wriggling, for the last minute Miss Edwards had told her information that interested her, "I'm on your side, Jessica, I am undercover at the school trying to catch the criminal, I wanted to tell you but things moved faster than I expected," she began, "I saw who took Andrew, I followed but lost them, I never imagined they were behind my house the whole time, I know you three were watching that car in your road so I watched from a distance hoping to get to them first."

Jessica eyed Miss Edwards suspiciously but before she could talk a voice from behind them said, "Now, what have we here?" Miss Edwards started to slip her left hand towards her jacket when the voice spoke again, "hands where I can see them, we don't want any accidents do we?" Jessica recognised the voice as the small man dressed in security clothing they had seen earlier.

Next to the small man was his larger friend, "I told you I heard something," he said.

"Yes, yes, I know," replied the small man irritably, "right, hands on heads and walk this way," he said pointing towards the warehouse using his small pistol as a pointer, "grab those bags," he said to the big man, who obeyed without talking.

Chloe watched from the end of the alley using the night gloom for cover, she edged closer and looked on as Miss Edwards and Jessica were led in to the warehouse, she went back to the milk crate under the window and slowly rose to the ledge, she saw the men take them to the back of the warehouse, unlock a door and push them in, the big man tossed the bags in to a corner and then followed into the room, a minute later he came out carrying a small revolver, radio and wallet in one hand and Jessica's phone in the other.

"Andrew!" exclaimed Jessica as she stumbled into the dimly lit storeroom, "are you okay?" she asked as he sat up.

"What is she doing here?" were Andrew's first words as he got to his feet.

Miss Edwards held her hands up as if in surrender, "It's okay, she's on our side," Jessica said then hurriedly she added, "She's a Spy as well."

"As well?" asked Miss Edwards looking puzzled ...

Chapter 20

Chloe pondered her next move but her thoughts were interrupted as car headlights came round the corner towards the warehouse, Chloe crouched in the darkness as the car came to a stop outside the main warehouse door, Chloe recognised the car *oh thank you* she thought as Mr Gunning stepped out of the car.

As Chloe got up to approach Mr Gunning the small man in the security uniform came rushing out of the door, she stopped dead in her tracks, *oh no* she breathed and stood almost statue-like and watched.

"Boss," started the small man, *boss* Chloe thought to herself, the small man continued, "we found two girls outside watching through the window and we have put them with that nosey kid in the back room."

"Well done," said Mr Gunning in reply, "that's all four nosey kids out of the way and us in the clear, the first lorry will be here soon so we better start moving the cars in preparation," he added, then they both went in to the warehouse.

Chloe stood there stunned, *Mr Gunning is the criminal* she thought *and we helped him whilst fishing out the Spy who is now trapped inside.*

Then it occurred to her, *they think I'm in there and the Spy Miss Edwards still has no idea who's behind all this*, she allowed herself a little smile and then made her way to the back of the warehouse, she looked around at what might be the back of the storeroom the others were locked in, then she noticed a small part of a window showing. Quietly she removed the barrels and planks in front of the small window, she rubbed the glass with her gloved hands, saw Jessica, Andrew and Miss Edwards and she gently tapped on the glass.

All three turned when they heard the tapping, Jessica put a hand over Andrew's mouth just in time as he began to call out Chloe's name, "Ssshh," said Jessica and Andrew nodded apologetically.

Miss Edwards made her way to the window and carefully reached up and opened it, "Chloe, you clever girl," she said "now, lower one of those planks through and we will climb out," she added.

Once all three were out of the storeroom Chloe looked at Miss Edwards, "We are so sorry, Miss Edwards," she whispered.

"Not your fault," she replied and smiled at the three friends, "and call me Steph." They all nodded and smiled back.

Chloe hugged Andrew, "I missed you," she said, Andrew smiled, but then Miss Edwards or Steph as she was now known interrupted.

"Jessica, I need you to go to my house, under the red plant pot is a key to the back door, go to the phone in the hall and on the pad is a number to call, tell them Code Alpha 90 and tell them where we are, then wait there."

Jessica nodded then trotted off towards the fence. "We need to delay the gang to allow my backup to arrive," said Steph to Chloe and Andrew.

"What shall we do?" asked Andrew.

Steph pondered this for a moment and then said, "I will stay at the front of the warehouse, there I can watch and see if I can get the opportunity try to overpower one of them, Andrew please go to the main entrance, you can direct my guys in, Chloe ..." but before she could say another word Chloe quickly spoke:

"I heard them say a lorry will be here soon to start taking the cars away."

"Okay, Andrew let the lorry come through if it gets here first but stay out of sight then shut the gates and block them with anything you can find and wait for our back up," said Steph, Andrew didn't hang around and practically sprinted off in to the darkness.

Chloe looked at Miss Edwards – Steph, she was still trying to process the name change and quietly asked, "And me?"

"Chloe," began Steph, "I might be asking a lot here but I would like your help dealing with these guys." Chloe just nodded, her voice a bit shaky she decided not to talk, and then they went towards the front of the warehouse each holding the end of a plank that Steph had said to pick up.

Slowly they edged around the front of the building, Steph crouched low and went the other side of the door, there she knelt opposite Chloe and indicated for her to lift the plank and sit against it, *oh clever* thought Chloe *they will trip over it when they come through the door*, inside they could hear cars being started and doors being opened and closed at the front of the warehouse and there they waited, Chloe was shaking in both terror and excitement. Seconds seemed like minutes, minutes like hours and Chloe's nerves were chewing at her insides.

She hoped they would be safe and that Jessica had put the call through, she looked at Steph who smiled reassuringly at her, then without warning sirens and lights burst on to the scene, within moments the two men in security uniforms came running towards the door to see what all the noise was about.

As they both came through the door they tripped over the plank and fell flat on their faces, by the time Chloe had rubbed her back from the impact Steph had raced over, kicking the small man in the face knocking him unconscious while taking his pistol and aiming it on the big man who put up no resistance. Chloe looked round expecting Mr Gunning – but nothing; she cautiously peered through the door but could only see cars, TVs and other stolen goods. Police swarmed everywhere, the two men had been picked up off the floor and Steph along with three others made their way in to the warehouse, slowly and with guns raised.

During the commotion Mr Gunning had gone to the storeroom, he kicked the door open and shouted, "Who's going to be a good hostage?" he soon realised the room was empty and he cursed, then he saw the plank going out of the window, he crawled up and made his way out.

Steph and her team searched the whole warehouse but could find no sign of Mr Gunning, they searched around and spread out, "We will make our way towards the fence," said Steph, "we can't let him get away now!" she added, all the while she directed the Police and other agents around.

Andrew came running round the corner, "So?" he said breathlessly.

"They have the two men but Mr Gunning has vanished," Chloe replied, Andrew shook his head and panted hard trying to get some air back in his lungs.

Mr Gunning had found a hole in the fence behind Miss Edwards – Steph's house, he looked back at the flashing lights and began to go through the gap, "Not this time," he said grinning to himself, a second later he found himself on the grass, circles of light flashed in his eyes and then he blacked out.

"That is for Kelly," said Jessica triumphantly, all the while she had watched and upon seeing Mr Gunning she hid in the darkness and then hit him on the head with the red plant pot with all her might.

Within minutes Steph and her team had handcuffed Mr Gunning whilst congratulating Jessica. Chloe and Andrew had made their way over. Steph told them what had happened, they laughed and hugged each other then Chloe stopped, looked around and said to her friends.

"Our teacher, the Spy, who would have thought it…"